ORCUS ON 34th LEVEL

Author: Jon Hook
Project Manager: Edwin Nagy
Editor: Jeff Harkness
Fifth Edition Conversion: Edwin Nagy
Art Director: Casey W. Christofferson
Cover Design: Jim Wampler
Front Cover Art: Adrian Landeros
Interior Art: Adrian Landeros, Faith Burgar
Layout: Suzy Moseby
Cartography: Dyson Logos

Frog God Games is:

Bill Webb, Matt Finch, Zach Glazar,
Charles A. Wright, Edwin Nagy,
Mike Badolato and John Barnhouse

ADVENTURES
WORTH
WINNING

ISBN: 978-1-6656-0089-7
5e PoD Softcover

Table of Contents

I want to thank the amazing and prolific cartographer, Dyson Logos, for the gift of his "The Lost Temple of Aphosh the Haunted" map. This map, and many more like it, are generously available for free from his website, DysonLogos.com. I made some very slight modifications to Dyson's original map, renamed it "The Candy Crypt", and used it in this adventure. If you enjoy Dyson's maps as much as I do, please consider supporting him by joining his Patreon.

I also want to thank the amazing James M. Spahn for creating such a wonderful toy in the Orcus' Claws and the Crueltide Elves. They were so much fun to play with; I hope my joy is felt by all who read or play this adventure. And finally, I want to say "thank you" to Edwin Nagy for inviting me to write this fun adventure. I was instantly captivated by this idea and it consumed for the twenty days it took me to write it. I was a man possessed by the raging and blood-drenched holiday spirit that oozes from Orcus' Claws. I am forever a changed man — somebody help me, please.

Enjoy!

—Jon Hook

ORCUS ON 34th LEVEL

BY JON HOOK
A 5e adventure for 4 to 6 Tier 2 adventurers

Orcus on 34th Level is a self-contained dungeon crawl adventure for 4–6 Tier 2 adventurers. Recently, the adventurers heard a rumor that jolly ol' Orcus' Claws is preparing to free his wife, Nohell Claws, from a remote dimension where she has been trapped for a thousand years. The ritual can be performed only when the constellation of Gorgon Major is in ascension and the Northern Azure Star shines over the village of Newville. That time is nigh, and if the adventurers fail to stop the ritual, then all *Nohell* is going to break loose!

BEGINNING THE ADVENTURE

For centuries, Orcus' Claws has pined for his one true soul-be-damned mate, a succubus known as Nohell. She is trapped in a null dimension, powerless to affect her own escape, spending a millennium in solitude. But now, as the time of her return draws near, Orcus' Claws has returned to the Candy Crypt, his lair deep within Mount Strumpet. While Orcus' Claws, his Crueltide elves, and the Naughty prepare the candy factory, Mr. Giggles, Claws' demonic astrologer, is conducting the summoning ritual.

The Candy Crypt is intended to be the 34th level of a mega-dungeon; insert it into any dungeon or run it as an isolated subterranean location. The adventurers either stumble upon the Candy Crypt by accident or they may be sent there to thwart Nohell's return. If a local noble hired them, they are promised a reward of 100 gp each. Additionally, each spellcaster will receive a scroll containing three rare spells, while everyone else is promised a magic weapon.

As the adventurers descend the spiral staircase that leads to **Room 1**, they hear music echoing through crypt. You are encouraged to play the instrumental song *Christmas Eve Sarajevo* by the Trans-Siberian Orchestra as the game is played. The author wrote lyrics for the song that can be heard echoing through the crypt as well. About one minute after the song begins, and just as the orchestra begins to swell, sing the following lyrics:

As he flew over the countryside

He listened for your cries,

When from a little village below

He heard the screams arise,

And there he dove to drink in the sight

And bathed in the blood of so many lives!

THE CANDY CRYPT

ROOM 1: WINDOW SHOPPING

The characters see an amazing sight as they enter this room, as their reflections repeat to infinity in every direction. Every character must make a DC 14 Wisdom saving throw to avoid being confused by the infinite reflections. On a failed save, the character suffers a –2 penalty on all attack rolls, skill checks, and saving throws while in this room.

Three reflection ghosts are trapped within this room, one inside each column. A fourth ghost used to be in the room, but one of the columns was destroyed, releasing the ghost and allowing it to escape. Each column is also linked to one of the room's four doors; if anyone whispers the secret name of the ghost tied to that particular door, it opens. If a ghost escapes the room, the associated door is permanently unlocked. While locked, nothing — no spell or blade — can harm or unlock the door.

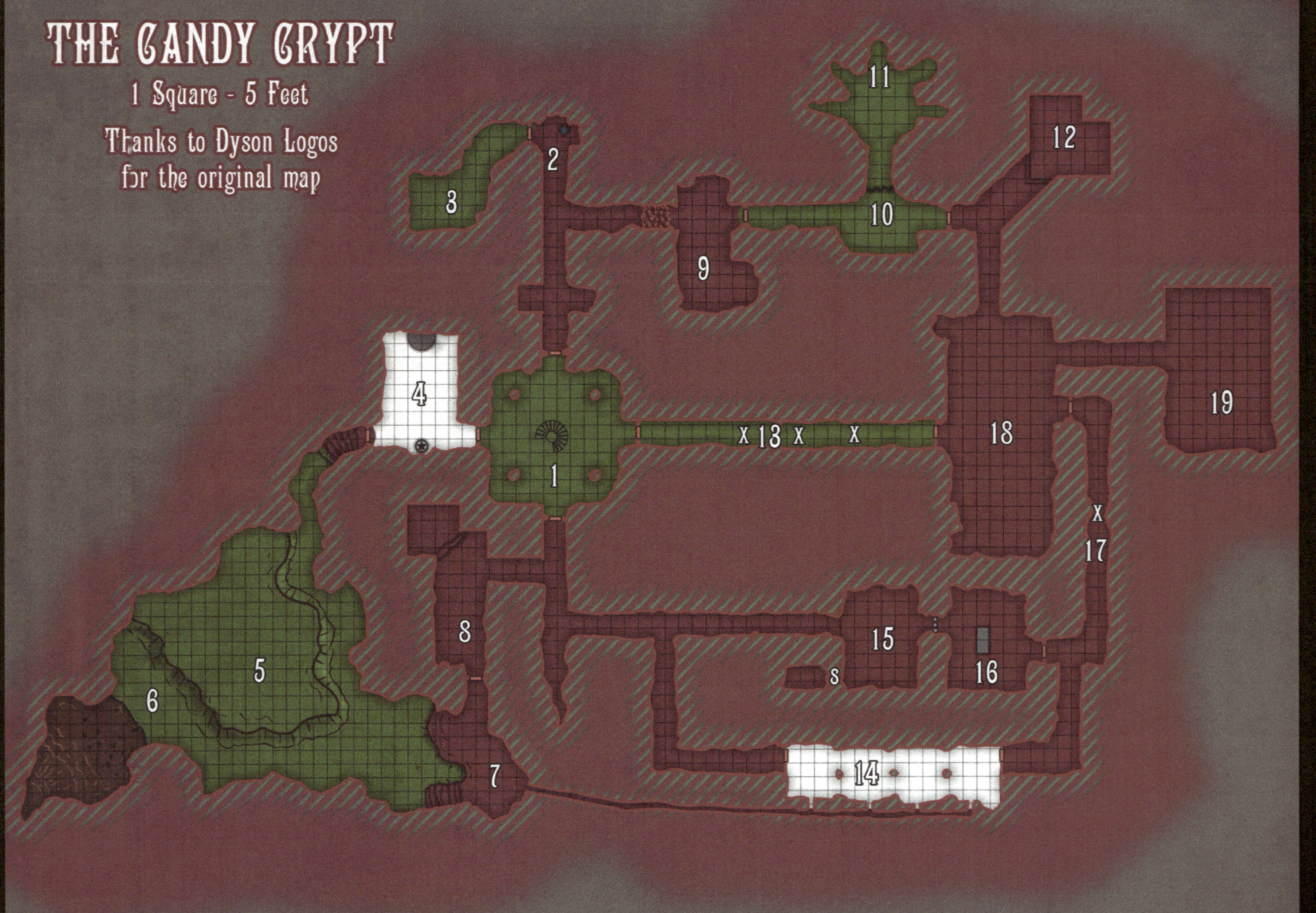

THE CANDY CRYPT
1 Square - 5 Feet
Thanks to Dyson Logos
for the original map
1
2
3
4
5
6
7
8
9
10
11
12
13
14
15
16
17
18
19
X
S

Reflection ghosts are invisible, immaterial, and intangible; they cannot be harmed, nor can they harm anyone as a ghost. However, a reflection ghost can manifest as a mirror image opposite any character that touches any reflective surface (walking does not count as touching a surface). Up to three mirrored manifestations can appear in this room, one from each intact column. A manifested reflection steps out of the mirror to battle its counterpart, fully equipped with all the character's gear and abilities, including hit points. If the mirror manifestation is destroyed, the reflection ghost returns to its column, until it manifests again.

Each column has 35 hit points and AC 16 and is linked to a different doorway. If a column is destroyed, it unlocks the connected doorway. The southwest column is linked to the door on the west wall, the northeast column to the door on the east wall, and the southeast column to the door on the south wall. The shattered northwest column was linked to the door on the north wall; that door unlocked when the column was destroyed. Unfortunately, destroying the columns also weakens the structural integrity of the chamber. The ceiling has a 20% cumulative chance of collapsing during any intense fighting for each column that is destroyed; if all three remaining columns are destroyed, there's an 80% chance of collapse (don't forget the 20% chance for the already destroyed column). Characters must make a DC 16 Dexterity saving throw to escape the room if the ceiling collapses. On a failed save, the character takes 10 (3d6) bludgeoning damage from falling stones and shards of mirror.

If the characters don't touch any reflective surfaces, it is possible for them to exit the room through the unlocked door in the north wall without manifesting any of the trapped reflection ghosts.

Room 2: Christmas Wishing Well

It is difficult to see the ceiling in this hallway; it's at least 30 feet high. Hundreds of iron chains ending with hooks dangle from the shadows. They slowly sway and jingle like bells as they clink against each other. Most of the hooks hang seven to eight feet off the floor. At the far end of the hall, a column of light illuminates a fountain of showering water.

This long hallway features two large niches near **Room 1**. Each niche is filled with chains dangling from the ceiling, with 3d4 corpses hanging from the hooks. The corpses are soft and wet, but instead of smelling like death, each one smells like strawberries, sugarplums, peaches, and honeysuckle. Each corpse is dressed in tattered undergarments; none of the corpses has any treasure.

The hallway features an eastward branch that caved in. Rubble completely blocks the passage, with 15 feet of debris separating this hallway from **Room 9**. Characters with stonecunning or an appropriate background can easily assess the rubble and see that with enough time it is possible to clear the way. It takes 10 hours for a single character to dig through the rubble; divide the time by the number of characters to determine how long it takes to clear the branch.

An eerie beam of light shines down from the ceiling directly over the fountain at the far northern end of the hallway. The marbled fountain has two basins: a small basin on a slim pedestal standing over a larger basin. Water cascades out of the upper basin and falls into the lower basin. A marble sculpture of crossed and bloodied candy canes stands upright in the center of the upper basin. The lower basin is lined with jagged, rusty nails, and its edge is stained dark brown with old blood. Swimming around inside the lower basin are small spheres of light that cast a dull yellow glow. The tiny balls of light move like goldfish.

The little glowing balls of light are nearly impossible to catch. The only way to catch a ball of light is for characters to stab their hands on the rusty nails, taking 2 (1d4) piercing damage, and then plunge their bleeding hands into the water. If this is done, a glowing ball swims directly into the open wound and buries itself in the character's flesh. The glowing ball is absorbed, and the character must make a DC 16 Charisma saving throw. Nothing happens on a successful save. If a character fails the saving throw, however, his or her alignment changes to Chaotic. If the character's alignment is already Chaotic, he or she is granted one wish (as per a *wish* spell). Any single Chaotic character may receive only one wish, and any attempt to gain a second results in 3d6 hooked chains grabbing the character and dealing 3 (1d6) piercing damage per hook. The character's body is lifted up and pulled into one of the niches near **Room 1**. The character's corpse is stored until it can be processed into candy.

Room 3: Dead Letter Office

The door to this chamber easily swings open. A rustling sound from beyond reminds you of the wind blowing through the trees. A large creature that looks more like a plant with four long and twisted tentacled limbs sits behind a desk covered in papers. The strange creature holds a quill curled within each appendage as it writes four letters simultaneously.

The creature's vegetable flesh appears long and rubbery; it is covered in leaves, thorns, and clusters of bright red berries. It stares at you from two hollow, coal-black eyes. Its wide toothy maw splits open as it yells, "I'm not ready yet!" The creature flips the desk and charges!

The creature is a **mistletroll** (see **Appendix A: New Creatures**). Its job is to write threatening letters to children promising that Orcus' Claws will sneak into their homes and steal them away from their parents to convert them into the Naughty so they can serve in Claws' Candy Crypt for all eternity. If the characters search the mistletroll's desk, they discover a small chest with 3d10 gp.

Room 4: Hot from the Oven

As soon as the door opens, you are greeted by the welcoming smell of warm bread baking. Most of the room is filled with low metal tables covered in flour. A life-sized statue of Orcus' Claws holding a reindeer's severed head stands on a short dais near the south wall, and a large clay oven dominates the north wall. The room is a beehive of activity by almost two dozen small gingersnap men. The cookie-men ignore you because they are intensely focused on their task of making more gingersnap men.

When the characters enter this room, 20 **gingersnap men** (see **Appendix A: New Creatures**) are busy making more cookie-men. Ten gingersnap men are working at the metal tables as they shape raw ginger cookie dough into new cookie-men; five gingersnap men are stirring a large bowl of raw cookie dough batter together in the northeast corner, and five gingersnap men are working in front of the oven. The oven workers insert raw, lifeless cookie-men and extract brand-new, fully baked and animated gingersnap men.

The clay oven is fueled by hellfire. Any non-gingersnap man that starts its turn in the oven or enters it for the first time on its turn must make a DC 14 Constitution saving throw. The creature takes 55 (10d10) fire damage on a failed saving throw and half as much on a success. Five new gingersnap men exit the oven every third combat round, even if they must crawl out on their own. The gingersnap men ignore the characters as long as they do not attempt to leave this room through the door that leads to the cavernous areas of **Rooms 5, 6,** and **7**, and as long as they do not interfere with their baking operation. The oven has a pair of metal doors that can be closed over the fiery opening. If the oven doors are closed and magically locked (by casting *arcane lock*, for example), the oven fires are snuffed out in 2d6 rounds.

The statue of Orcus' Claws has a pair of precious rubies for eyes. Each ruby is worth 150 gp. The statue is magically trapped. If anyone touches either ruby eye, that person is teleported into the oven. *Detect magic* informs the spellcaster that the ruby eyes are magically trapped but does not reveal the exact nature of the trap. *Dispel magic* can disarm the trap for up to 10 minutes. The spellcaster must succeed on a DC 15 ability check with their spellcasting ability. The trap was originally cast by Orcus' Claws' astrologer, Mr. Giggles.

Room 5: Ice Cream Quarry

The temperature drops dramatically as you enter this cavernous area, causing your breath to exhale as a cloud of warm vapor. The walls and floors sparkle with ice crystals, and the entire cavern is composed of ice cream. You see a quarry pit filled with gingersnap men toiling away as they excavate chunks of chocolate ore and veins of caramel from the ice cream walls. Flying over the gingersnap men, directing their work, is a trio of large demonic-looking snowy owls.

The gingersnap men baked in **Room 4** are sent to the ice cream quarry to work. **Gingersnap men** (see **Appendix A: New Creatures**) are a mindless race; it is thus impossible for the characters to stoke a rebellion in them. When the adventurers enter, 15 gingersnap men are working in the quarry. The gingersnap men ignore the characters; they attack only if their work is interrupted. On the other hand, the three demonic owls, also known as **kringkuks** (see **Appendix A: New Creatures**), attack the adventurers on sight. The kringkuks have a quota of ore to collect, and they do not allow the characters to threaten their work schedule.

The gingersnap men collect ore and place it in carts that are wheeled to **Room 7** for processing. One of the carts currently parked in an alcove along the eastern wall of the cavern contains some other ore the gingersnap men discovered, including 3d20 ingots of gold "*sprinkles*." Each ingot is worth 10 gp. An intelligent dagger named *Frost Fang* (see **Appendix B: New Magic Items**) is also in the cart; the blade was unable to communicate with the mindless gingersnap men. The gingersnap men also found a large magical gem known as an *ice storm sapphire* (see **Appendix B: New Magic Items**).

Ice Cream Caves

The Ice Cream Caves are extremely cold. The characters must make a DC 14 Constitution saving throw for every half hour they spend in the frozen caves. On a failed save, the character takes 2 (1d4) cold damage and has their movement slowed by 10 feet while in the cave.

Room 6: Chocolate Falls

The cavern's ceiling here is 60 feet high. From high above, a fountain of chocolate spews out and falls into a pool of chocolate below. Several large chunks of dark chocolate fudge float in the pool of light-brown milk chocolate.

None of the gingersnap men works near the chocolate pool. Several large boulder-like scoops of ice cream near the pool provide cover for the characters if they choose to hide near the pool. Characters who drink the liquid chocolate satiate their hunger for a full day. If the characters spend more than five minutes near the pool's edge, the **chocolate pudding** (see **Appendix A: New Creatures**) emerges and attacks.

Room 7: Ore Processing

The gingersnap men push carts of candied ore to a basket at the base of the cliff wall below the processing station. The gingersnap men transfer the ore from the cart to the basket, which is then pulled up to the processing station by Crueltide elves. The elves unload the basket, sort the ore, and load it onto conveyer belts that carry the ore through a small tunnel in the eastern wall.

Eight **Crueltide elves** (see **Appendix A: New Creatures**) sing the haunting carol the adventurers first heard as they descended into **Room 1**. The elves are sorting the ore mined by the gingersnap men into different piles. The ore is loaded onto a conveyer belt system that runs through small tunnels dug through the east wall to deliver the ore to the Bittersweet Treats chamber (**Room 14**).

The conveyer belt tunnel is exceedingly small; only a Small or smaller creature can fit through the tunnel. The tunnel is incredibly claustrophobic, and anyone attempting to travel through the conveyer belt tunnel must make a DC 13 Constitution saving throw every 30 feet or lose 1 hit point due to asphyxiation.

The Crueltide elves are focused on their work and most likely do not notice the characters until they enter their work area. Each Crueltide elf carries 1d2 items from the **Crueltide Contraptions Chart** within a *bag of limited holding* (see **Appendix B: New Magic Items**), a pocketful of 2d6 miniature candy canes, and a dagger.

Room 8: Bubblegum Refuse

A half dozen shovel-wielding **Crueltide elves** (see **Appendix A: New Creatures**) are working in this room. Several piles of broken toys, pieces of warped candy, crumbled cookies, and other heaping piles of junk are scattered about the room. The demonic elves are shoveling the debris into a sunken area in the northwest corner of the room where a large pink sphere is located in the lower section of the room. The rubbery-looking sphere warbles as the junk the elves keep shoveling penetrates its elastic skin.

This is the disposal room. Anything broken or no longer useful is chucked into the **bubblegum sphere** (see **Appendix A: New Creatures**) for the creature to consume. Each Crueltide elf in this room carries a shovel, a dagger, and a small *bag of limited holding* (see **Appendix B: New Magic Items**) containing 1d2 Crueltide contraptions (see **Crueltide Contraptions Table**). Many precious items were discarded by mistake; each character who searches through the piles of refuse may roll once on the **Random Treasure Table** below. Each treasure can be found only once; reroll all duplicate results.

The large pink bubblegum sphere is ravenous and must be continually fed by the Crueltide elves. If the feeding ceases, the bubblegum sphere lifts off from the dais it is sitting on and floats into the room to attack anyone threatening its constant food supply.

1d12	Result
1	A small sack with 3d10 gold coins.
2	A quiver with 2d4 arrows. Each arrowhead glows a soft green. Each enchanted arrow bestows a +2 bonus to hit and damage rolls, but this quiver is in the junkpile for a reason: The arrows are unstable. Each time one of these arrows is nocked and drawn, roll 1d6: On a 1, the arrow explodes in the archer's hands and inflicts 5 (1d6 + 2) force damage to the archer and destroys the bow.
3	A small sack with 2d3 tiny gemstones (diamonds, emeralds, rubies, and sapphires); each gem is worth 50 gp.
4	A small figurine of a silver eagle — a *figurine of wondrous power* (silver eagle), see **Appendix B: New Magic Items**.
5	A small locked box from which leaks thin tendrils of vapor that have an acrid, electrical smell. The lock is not trapped, but the object inside — a large diamond containing an enchanted lightning bolt — is unstable. If the box is opened, the lightning bolt automatically discharges. Everyone within 10 feet must make a DC 15 Dexterity saving throw, taking 10 (3d6) lightning damage on a failure or half as much on a success. Once the lightning bolt discharges, the diamond is no longer enchanted but is still worth 600 gp.
6	A small sack with 2d12 gold coins and a golden ring etched with an image of a skeleton. It is a *ring of X-ray vision*.
7	A filthy and stained burlap sack that stinks of rot and decay. Inside is a thick skeletal left hand covered in moldy, green-gray flesh. Each of the four fingers stands up and erect, and the thumb is tucked in close to the palm. Each of the four fingertips has a small black wick showing. It is a *hand of glory* (see **Appendix B: New Magic Items**).
8	A shabby, floppy purple hat with two white feathers. It is a *charming chapeau* (see **Appendix B: New Magic Items**).
9	A small velvet sack containing 2d10 enchanted six-sided *chaos dice* (see **Appendix B: New Magic Items**).
10	A small sack appears with 6d6 tiny gemstones (diamond, emeralds, rubies, and sapphires), each worth 20 gp.
11	A hollowed-out ram's horn fashioned into a war horn. It is a *berserker* horn (see **Appendix B: New Magic Items**).
12	A coal-black warhammer appears. It is *Cruuf'xk's Warhammer* (see **Appendix B: New Magic Items**).

Room 9: Contraption Factory

From the hallway outside, it is easy to hear the *ting-ting* of tiny hammers crafting deadly toys. Inside the room, it is dark and poorly lit. Working in the room are 10 Crueltide elves, each seated at a table with a pair of low-burning candles providing the lighting needed for their tasks. The room is old — ancient even — and the ceiling sags, a portion of the north wall has fallen in, and a corridor to the west has collapsed and is full of rubble.

The elderly Crueltide elves (as **Crueltide elves** with Challenge 0 and 1 hit point, see **Appendix A: New Creatures**) in this chamber seem as ancient and feeble as the room itself. None of them has the strength or stamina to battle the adventurers, but seven new experimental contraptions are ready to defend their creators: the meka-men! Each **meka-man** (see **Appendix A: New Creatures**) stands seven feet tall and is made of iron. Their bodies are covered in filigree and fancy sculpting details, and they are painted in bright colors with rosy red cheeks and big eyes. Four of the meka-men wield swords, while three hold wands.

Each geriatric Crueltide elf has only 1 hit point and no armor; they are easily slain. Anyone searching the room may roll 1d6: on a 1–4, they find broken and incomplete contraptions; on a 5–6, they find one contraption (roll on the **Crueltide Contraptions Table**).

Room 10: Lost Souls

The tortured moans and cries of prisoners fill this room. A curtain of chains separates this room from a corridor to the north, and an open sarcophagus positioned above a bed of red-hot coals is along the south wall. Exhausted and defeated prisoners are shackled to the walls. Their torturers are a band of twisted people with horns, demonic grins, hooved feet, and stinger tails. One of them sees your crew of adventurers and says, "Oh look! Fresh meat!"

The thirteen demonic creatures are known as the **Naughty** (see **Appendix A: New Creatures**). This room is where they torture their hapless victims. They place a prisoner into the sarcophagus and then fill it with candy canes. The coals under the sarcophagus are stoked until the candy canes melt. The Naughty then remove the candied golem and place it in **Room 11** for safekeeping. If rescued, the five prisoners can help the characters as hirelings fighting for their freedom, and if a character dies, a prisoner can serve as a replacement. The insanity and torture the prisoners endured has turned them all into **berserkers**.

Room 11: Sweet Tomb

This circular chamber has a 25-foot-high domed ceiling and five niches evenly spaced around the northern hemisphere of the room. A large sarcophagus is within each niche. The lid of each sarcophagus is sculpted to resemble a giant candy-jellied bear, and each is painted a different color: blue, red, yellow, green, and purple. A two-foot-diameter red-and-white striped orb hangs from a short chain in the center of the domed ceiling. The orb spins slowly.

As the characters enter this chamber, the spinning orb begins to glow with an internal white light that pulses like a heartbeat. The orb returns to a dormant mode when no one is in the room. Each jelly-bear sarcophagus contains 2d3 + 1 **candied golems** (see **Appendix A: New Creatures**) that the Naughty created in **Room 10**. They are piled in the crypts like cordwood. Each candied golem is in a state of suspended animation; the key to their animation is slowly spinning on the ceiling.

The orb fires a bolt of lightning at two sarcophagi as it is able. When the lightning strikes, one of the candied golems inside each sarcophagus animates. The golems slide open their tombs and lumber out to attack.

The secret to this room is to destroy the **spinning orb** (see **Appendix A: New Creatures**). Without it, the candied golems cannot be reanimated.

Room 12: Demonic Choir

The music heard throughout this candied crypt grows louder as you approach this chamber. As you enter, you discover a 13-piece demonic orchestra, but each humanoid musician is skinless, and their instruments are abominations constructed out of bones. Standing on the small stage is the choir, a quartet of demons singing in perfect harmony.

As noted in **Beginning the Adventure** above, remind the players about the music and the singing that echoes through this dungeon. The orchestra is impervious to harm. If a musician is slain, it just stands back up during the next combat round to continue playing its instrument. If its instrument is destroyed, it automatically knits back together so it can be played again. The musicians have no action other than playing music.

The four members of the choir are **erinyes** demons. At least one erinyes must continue singing to maintain control of the orchestra. If all four erinyes are destroyed, their grip on the orchestra is released. As soon as the last erinyes dies, the orchestra changes its tune and begins playing a melody that sounds like the opening theme music for the *Tales from the Crypt* television series. The new song also echoes throughout the Candy Crypt. The orchestra's musicians despise Orcus' Claws, so the new song bestows a +1 to-hit bonus and a +1 bonus to saving throws the the player characters while it is playing.

Area 13: Dangerous Hall

The floor and ceiling of this long hallway are painted a bright white. The walls are decorated with brightly painted frescos depicting the mighty Orcus' Claws visiting merry mayhem on hapless villagers.

A new fresco image is found every 10 feet along the hallway. Starting at **Room 1** (fresco 1 on table below) and running to **Room 18** (fresco 10), the images depicted along the hallway are:

Fresco	Description
1	Orcus' Claws driving his sleigh through a pale evening sky filled with black stars.
2	Orcus' Claws looking jolly as his reindeer are slaughtering and eating frightened villagers.
3	Orcus' Claws stuffing frightened children into his bulging sack.
4	Orcus' Claws relaxing and reclining in a comfy chair as he pulls a strip of meat off a bone with his teeth. The foot on the leg is still wearing a pink bunny slipper. Claws has a glass of milk in his other hand. (Trapped)
5	Orcus' Claws looking over his shoulder to smile and wink at the viewer as he warms his hands over a burning holiday tree with a restrained family tied to the trunk.
6	Orcus' Claws placing bloodstained weapons decorated in colorful ribbons and bows under the holiday tree. A severed hand lies nearby in a pool of bright red blood. (Trapped)
7	Orcus' Claws in full belly laugh as a trio of animated dolls with knives surround and menacingly close in on a frightened little girl.
8	Orcus' Claws placing a large candy cane into a stocking nailed to a fireplace mantel, but the stocking is already bulging and overstuffed with creepy crawling insects. A wet eyeball with a few inches of optical nerve sits on the mantel near the stocking. (Trapped)
9	Orcus' Claws walking back toward his sleigh. Two crying and defeated kids are slung over one shoulder, and he drags a third kid behind him by the hair.
10	Orcus' Claws and his sleigh of flying reindeer silhouetted against a full moon as a village burns below them.

The hallway is trapped at Frescos 4, 6, and 8:

Fresco No. 4 Trap: Anyone stepping in front of this fresco must make a DC 14 Dexterity saving throw or fall 10 feet into a 20-foot-by-20-foot room, taking 3 (1d6) bludgeoning damage and landing prone. Three **jackals of darkness** (see **Appendix A: New Creatures**) with glowing red eyes stalk the room and instantly attack anyone who falls into their den. The cover of the pit can be see with a successful DC 18 Wisdom (Perception) check.

Fresco No. 6 Trap: A huge axe blade swings on a pendulum between the walls to strike at anyone stepping in front of this fresco. The axe makes an attack at +8 to hit and does 9 (2d8(slashing damage on a hit. The frescos conceal the slit from which the pendulum swings, but a successful DC 18 Wisdom (Perception) check reveals the concealed opening. After the blade swings, dozens of poisoned needles rain down from the ceiling. All creatures in a 10-foot area in front of the fresco must make a DC 15 Dexterity saving throw or be struck by 1d4 + 2 poisoned needles. The needles do 1 (1d3) piercing damage each, and the creature must make a DC 15 Constitution saving throw. On a failure, the creature drops to 0 hit points in 1d6 rounds, while on a success it takes 7 (2d6) poison damage.

Fresco No. 8 Trap: The 10-foot-by-10-foot section of floor in front of this fresco is thin and easily breaks away. The trap can be detected with a successful DC 18 Intelligence (Investigation) check while examining the floor. Anyone stepping in front of this fresco sinks into a pit filled with insects (centipedes, millipedes, spiders, beetles, cockroaches, worms, etc.). The pit is 30 feet deep, and it's filled nearly to the top with insects. Because of the insects' constant squirming, anyone caught in the pit begins to quickly sink and drown.

Characters must succeed on a DC 15 Strength (Athletics) check each round to "swim" through the insects and keep their head above the squirming mass. Insect bites inflict 1 piercing damage each round to characters who make their Athletics check but remain in the pit. Anyone who fails their check submerges and takes 3 (1d6) piercing damage each round. They can succeed on a check on the next round to claw their way back to the surface. Characters who fail three checks in a row drown in the insects. Due to their massive numbers, weapons have no effect on the pit full of insects.

This room is a beehive of activity. Raw candy ore is delivered on a series of conveyer belts. The ore is plucked from the belts, torn and crushed into smaller bits, and then mixed with other components to create pounds of tasty holiday treats. Four large tentacled monstrosities are hard at work in this candy factory; each of their tentacles is decorated in little silver bells that jangle as they work. If the legends are to be believed, before you is a quartet of jingle grells!

The **jingle grells** (see **Appendix A: New Creatures**) are focused on their work, and they attack the characters only if they are attacked first or if any character enters their zone. Each jingle grell works in a 20-foot-by-20-foot zone separated by a thick column. At the rear of each zone, a narrow passage leads to the conveyor belt from **Room 7**. Some of the ore is automatically scraped off the belt as it passes each location, making a slowly growing pile for jingle grells to use.

If the jingle grells are defeated, the characters discover stacks and stacks of boxed candied treats and the corpse of an unfortunate soul who lost his life to the jingle grells long ago.

The corpse is that of Montague J. Sebastian, a famed astrologer, sage, and wizard who vanished many years ago. It seems that the characters have solved the riddle of his disappearance. Sebastian's corpse holds the following treasures: *boots of elvenkind, cloak of elvenkind*, a *ring of protection*, a *staff of power*, an ivory and mahogany *+2 crossbow* with a dozen silver bolts (+2 / +4 versus undead), a *wand of lightning bolts*, a small chest with 3d20 + 20 gp and 2d8 precious gems (40 gp each), and his spellbook, which contains 1d6 + 2 1st-level spells, 1d4 + 2 2nd-level spells, 1d3 + 1 3rd-level spells, 1d3 4th-level spells, and a 5th-level spell.

Room 15: Storage

Life-sized wooden dolls fill this large chamber. None of the wooden dolls is painted or decorated; instead, they either have a light pine varnish or a darker oak, pecan, or maple stain. Some of the wooden dolls are more than six feet tall, while others are only three feet tall. Some are thin and svelte, while others are broad and heavy. None of the dolls appears to have a definitive gender, but some seem vaguely masculine, some appear more feminine, and a few are genderless. This room is so full of wooden dolls that it is impossible to move through it without pushing past and brushing up against two or more dolls with every step taken.

The wooden dolls are the remains of adventurers who attempted to plunder Orcus' Claws' Candy Crypt. The unfortunate adventurers were transformed into wooden dolls by the bite of a creature known as a **pheasatrice** (as **cockatrice** except victims are turned to wood rather than petrified). A secret coop of six pheasatrices is hidden in the southwest corner of the room. Once characters start moving through the room, the sound of the wooden dolls knocking against each other alerts the creatures that prey has entered their lair.

The Puzzle: The east corridor leads to the office (**Room 16**), but a portcullis blocks the corridor. A manual wheel to lift the portcullis is in **Room 16**, but it cannot be seen or operated by anyone inside **Room 15**. Instead, the storage room has a magical puzzle lock that can raise the portcullis. The east corridor is gothic in design, with a peaked arch that is 12 feet high at the summit. Unique clay tiles outline the arch. The tile at the peak of the arch is embossed with a star-shaped ridge, and all the tiles that outline the rest of the archway have a gutter that flows down to a pair of small holes in the floor. Any liquid poured onto the star-embossed tile at the peak splits into two channels and flows down either side of the archway, where it eventually drains into the holes on the floor. Closer inspection of the star-embossed tile reveals the ridge has an egg-shaped background. The enchanted portcullis is impervious to magical and physical harm and cannot be lifted.

The Solution: The characters need to smash a pheasatrice egg against the star-embossed tile at the peak of the archway. The bloodied yolk then oozes down both sets of guttered tiles on either side of the archway and drains into the holes on the floor. Throwing an egg at the star-embossed tile requires a successful ranged attack against AC 19. One character could also lift another onto their shoulders to smash the egg against the tile by hand. When the egg cracks and the yolk spills down the gutters, each tile illuminates in a golden yellow light. Manually cracking two eggs into the drains at the base of the arch does not raise the portcullis.

Medium characters must squeeze while in the room because of the multitude of wooden dolls, and the entire area is difficult terrain for all characters. The wall concealing the pheasatrices' coop has gaps in the bricks that the creatures can move through. Knocking down the wall of loosely stacked bricks exposes the coop. The six pheasatrices typically leave the coop one at a time to attack intruders, but if the wall concealing their coop is knocked down, all remaining pheasatrices attack. The coop contains 3d6 pheasatrice eggs, each worth 250 gp to an alchemist.

ROOM 16: THE OFFICE

The large bloodstained stone altar in the center of the room is being used as a desk. Four torches on eight-foot-tall iron rods are positioned near the corners of the desk. A dour-looking human wearing expensive robes sits at the desk and scratches at a scroll with a quill in his hand.

A wheel that operates the portcullis in the corridor leading to the storage area (**Room 15**) is in the northwest corner of the room. The gentleman introduces himself as Sir Ramasin Kalam, a demi-knight, scribe, and oracle tasked with managing the daily operations of the Candy Crypt. In truth, Kalam is a **rakshasa** with a scimitar named *Hawkeye* (see **Appendix B: New Magic Items**). Kalam does not want to be disturbed. He refuses to help anyone who calls out to him from the portcullis, and he becomes terribly angry if anyone enters his room. While in his human guise, Kalam appears to have a great tiger tattoo across his chest and back. When he transforms into his true rakshasa form, the tattoo ripples, envelops his whole body, and he manifests as a ferocious tiger-man.

If Kalam is destroyed and the desk searched, the characters discover a scroll titled, *Opening the Way through Gorgon Major* (see **side box**). The scroll details the ritual required to open a gateway for Nohell Claws to return to this plane of existence, as well as a separate ritual for closing and sealing the gate. The scroll can be read by spellcasters and elves. The Gorgon Major gate can be closed only by using this scroll. In addition to the scroll, the adventurers discover a *luckstone* being used as a paperweight, a leather-bound book written by Sir Ramasin Kalam titled, *Eye of the Tiger: A Memoir* (it is a *tome of clear though*), a *crystal ball* on a small bronze tripod, and a small chest with 3d10 + 20 gp and 2d12 small gems worth 30 gp each.

OPENING THE WAY THROUGH GORGON MAJOR (SCROLL)

This scroll contains the ritual needed to open or close the Gorgon Major gate. For the characters to use the scroll to close the gate, one character must maintain concentration (as if concentrating on a spell) for a total of five rounds (not necessarily consecutive) while reading from the scroll before Mr. Giggles does the same. In the event of a tie, Mr. Giggles wins. If the Gorgon Major gate is successfully opened, Nohell Claws steps through. See the Observatory (**Room 19**) for more details.

AREA 17: THE VOID

The hallway narrows to only five feet wide for a distance of 10 feet. The cobblestone floor is unchanged in the short stretch of hallway, but the walls and ceiling are dramatically different. The walls and ceiling are black as pitch, and they seem to rapidly vibrate with a subsonic hum. Your hairs rise into gooseflesh as you draw closer. Your gut tells you that something is very wrong with the walls in that part of the hallway, something otherworldly.

The disturbing portion of the hallway is a wound, an open scar to a plane of chaos that hungers for life and that literally attempts to grab anyone who passes through the narrow corridor. As the characters move through the narrow corridor, 1d3 + 1 arms and tentacles of various sizes and shapes reach from the void to grab each of them. They act on Initiative 20, losing ties. Each appendage makes an attack at +7 to hit. On a success, the target is grappled (escape DC 14 + 2 for each appendage above one that has grappled the target). The first round an appendage starts its turn with a creature grappled, that creature is pulled halfway into the void. The second round the appendage start its turn with the same creature grappled, that creature is pulled through the wall and lost forever. A creature that is not grappled may attempt a DC 14 (+2 per additional appendage) Strength check to pull a grappled creature free of the appendages.

ROOM 18: THE THRONE ROOM

This room is enormous, with a ceiling that is 30 feet high. Three huge 15-foot-diameter chandeliers are evenly spaced down the length of the room, each casting a sickly yellow light into every corner of the room. A huge line of seemingly mindless people is queued in a zig-zag pattern that runs the full length of the room. The procession begins in a niche in the northwest corner of the room, where an open dimensional door allows the people to slowly shuffle through. The line ends at the southern end of the room, where jolly ol' Orcus' Claws sits upon a throne of bones. The bones are festively painted red, white, and green.

The belly laugh of **Orcus' Claws** (see **Appendix A: New Creatures**) is more of a "Har-har-harrr" than a "Ho-ho-hooo!" Claws has delegated the task of summoning his beloved Nohell Claws to his able astrologer, Mr. Giggles, which allows Claws the time to convert more damned souls into his legion of the Naughty. It takes three combat rounds of Claws whispering into the ear of a soulless wretch to transform it into one of the Naughty. Claws cannot belly laugh and whisper to the soulless at the same time. When the characters enter the room, Claws has already created four of the **Naughty** (see **Appendix A: New Creatures**). Six **Crueltide elves** and 10 **brownie bites** (see **Appendix A: New Creatures** for both) manage the line of soulless wretches. The wretches only have 1 hit point each and AC 10. They feel no pain and take no interest in anything or anyone around them.

The portal from which the procession of soulless wretches emerge leads to a level deep within the Abyss. If the characters choose to escape the Candy Crypt by traveling to the Abyss, then you should close the curtains on this adventure and prepare something for them to explore in the Abyss.

If he senses his end is near, Orcus' Claws teleports away in a cloud of fire and brimstone to a secret lair deep within the Abyss to recuperate. If his throne is searched, the characters discover a large chest hidden in a secret compartment under the seat. The chest is trapped and releases a cloud of poisonous gas in a 10-foot radius unless the trap is successfully disarmed. Each creature in the area must make a DC 16 Constitution saving throw, taking 14 (3d8) acid damage on a failure or half as much on a success as the gas causes a victim's flesh to violently blister and pop. The trap can be found with a successful DC 15 Wisdom (Perception) check and disarmed with a successful DC 18 Dexterity check with thieves' tools.

The chest contains 4d6 x 50 gp, 3d12 large gems worth 125 gp each, a black silk sack containing a *robe of eyes*, a pan flute made from human bones (*pipes of the sewers*), and a stone earth elemental figurine designed to hold incense sticks (a *stone of controlling earth elementals*).

ROOM 19: THE OBSERVATORY

This large room has a domed ceiling enchanted to display a dark sky full of stars in motion. The stars make up the amazing constellation of Gorgon Major as it rises above a vortex gateway of swirling energy on the east wall. The silhouette of a bat-winged woman with long flowing hair is fighting her way through the vortex to enter this chamber. Standing before the vortex is a dwarf with fluffy pink hair and a beard, and he wears a robe covered in gumdrops. The dwarf is raising his arms toward the vortex and chanting at the portal. As you enter the room, a host of demonic minions in the room turn to face you!

A lot is happening in this room, so take careful note of all the moving parts. The four main aspects of this room are:

1) Mr. Giggles needs to maintain concentration for five total rounds to finish opening the Gorgon Major gate;

2) A character needs to maintain concentration for five total while reading from the scroll to permanently close the Gorgon Major gate;

3) The horde of demonic minions is ready to battle the characters;

4) Nohell Claws might enter the room and engage the characters.

Mr. Giggles is not a true dwarf; he is actually a dwarf-like demon known as a **faerhle** (see **Appendix A: New Creatures**). Each round, if Mr. Giggles attempts to maintain concentration on his spell to open the portal.

A character reading from the *Opening the Way through Gorgon Major* scroll (see sidebox in the Office [**Room 16**]) may also attempt to maintain concentration to close the Gorgon Major gate.

The demonic minions in the room are **arauks** (see **Appendix A: New Creatures**) and, as luck would have it, there are the same number of arauks as there are characters. Each arauk carries four kukri shortswords.

Nohell Claws is a unique **succubus/incubus** demon. She is ample and curvy and the bride of Orcus' Claws. She has been trapped in a realm beyond the stars for a millennium. Finally, the stars are right, and a way can be opened for her return. Nohell can sense the characters fighting against her return, and it enrages her. If she successfully escapes her exile, she exacts her wrath upon the characters.

Final Conflict?

Ideally, the conflict in the Observatory (**Room 19**) is the conclusion of this dungeon delve. Assuming the characters defeat Mr. Giggles and prevent Nohell Claws from entering this realm (or if she does enter and they defeat her), then the looming threat in this adventure has been resolved and you can "fade to black" with the players having had a satisfying end to the game. However, it is also likely that the characters did not fully explore the Candy Crypt before the finale occurred. So what should you do if your players want to continue exploring this sugar and spice hellscape?

The denizens of the Candy Crypt are anxiously awaiting the coming of Nohell Claws, and they sense if she is repelled or defeated. In that case, if the orchestra is still under the thumb of the choir of erinyes demons, then the music changes in pitch and tone to something more somber and dire. This new melody of melancholy grants all creatures native to the Candy Crypt a +2 bonus to hit and damage rolls. The foul creatures that dwell within the Candy Crypt have no reason to retreat or flee from the invasive adventurers.

THE CANDY CRYPT

1 Square - 5 Feet

Thanks to Dyson Logos
for the original map

11
12
10
9
13
18
19
17
15
16
14

APPENDIX A: NEW CREATURES

Monsters found in this merry adventure that are not in the Fifth Edition SRD are listed below.

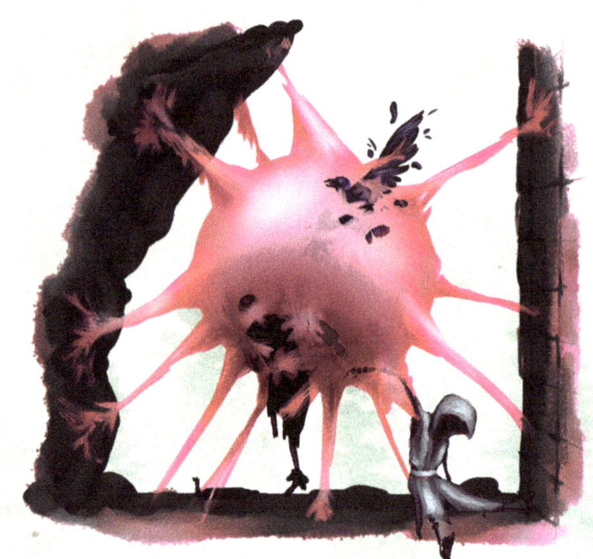

BROWNIE BITES

Tiny fiend, chaotic neutral

Armor Class 20 (natural armor)
Hit Points 5 (2d4)
Speed fly 60 ft.

STR	DEX	CON	INT	WIS	CHA
8 (−1)	20 (+5)	10 (+0)	10 (+0)	12 (+1)	8 (−1)

Saving Throws Dex +7
Senses blindsight 30 ft., passive Perception 11
Languages —
Challenge 1/8 (25 XP)

Flyby. The Brownie Bites doesn't provoke opportunity attacks when it flies out of an enemy's reach.

ACTIONS

Bite. *Melee Weapon Attack:* +7 to hit, reach 5 ft., one target. *Hit:* 7 (1d4 + 5) piercing damage.

Brownie bites are eyeless, fist-size balls of fur. Half their body is a mouth filled with rows of razor-sharp teeth. They have a pair of dragonfly-like wings that allow them to flit and buzz around at amazing speeds. They are incredibly difficult to hit due to their uncanny speed.

BUBBLEGUM SPHERE

Medium aberration, unaligned

Armor Class 11
Hit Points 39 (6d8 + 12)
Speed fly 10 ft.

STR	DEX	CON	INT	WIS	CHA
16 (+3)	12 (+1)	14 (+2)	3 (−4)	10 (+0)	7 (−2)

Damage Immunities fire, lightning
Condition Immunities blinded, charmed, exhaustion, frightened, prone, stunned
Senses blindsight 60 ft., passive Perception 10
Languages —
Challenge 2 (450 XP)

Sticky. A creature who hits the bubblegum sphere with a melee weapon attack must succeed on a DC 14 Strength saving throw or their weapon becomes stuck to the bubblegum sphere. The weapon can be retrieved with a successful unarmed melee attack against the bubblegum sphere followed by a successful DC 14 Strength check.

ACTIONS

Stick. *Melee Weapon Attack:* +5 to hit, reach 5 ft., one target. *Hit:* the target is grappled and paralyzed. At the beginning of each of the bubblegum sphere's turns, the target takes 5 (2d4) acid damage. Another creature can use an action to attempt a DC 15 Strength (Athletics) check to pull the target free, ending the effects on the target on a success.

Bubblegum spheres are a spherical mass of gelatinous polymer, with an outer surface that is gummy and sticky. Contrary to popular belief, they are not hollow on the inside.

Candied Golem

Large construct, unaligned

Armor Class 14 (natural armor)
Hit Points 85 (10d10 + 30)
Speed 30 ft.

STR	DEX	CON	INT	WIS	CHA
18 (+4)	12 (+1)	16 (+3)	4 (−3)	12 (+1)	7 (−2)

Damage Immunities piercing, slashing
Condition Immunities charmed, frightened, petrified, stunned, unconscious
Senses darkvision 60 ft., passive Perception 11
Languages understands Abyssal but can't speak
Challenge 3 (700 XP)

Magic Immunity. The candied golem is immune to all magical spells and effects except those that cause fire damage.

Actions

Multiattack. The candied golem makes two fist attacks.
Fist. *Melee Weapon Attack:* +7 to hit, reach 5 ft., one target. *Hit:* 13 (2d8 + 4) bludgeoning damage.

Chocolate Pudding

Large ooze, unaligned

Armor Class 11 (natural armor)
Hit Points 39 (6d10 + 6)
Speed 20 ft.

STR	DEX	CON	INT	WIS	CHA
15 (+2)	10 (+0)	12 (+1)	3 (−4)	8 (−1)	2 (−4)

Damage Immunities bludgeoning, piercing, and slashing from nonmagical attacks
Condition Immunities blinded, charmed, frightened, grappled, prone, restrained, unconscious
Senses blindsight 60 ft.
Languages —
Challenge 1 (200 XP)

Water Vulnerability. For every 1 gallon of water splashed on the chocolate pudding, it takes 1d6 cold damage.

Actions

Envelope. *Melee Weapon Attack:* +4 to hit, reach 5 ft., one target. *Hit:* the target is grappled (escape DC 14) and begins to suffocate. If a victim dies from the suffocation, its body is digested and converted into large chunks of dark fudge and the chocolate pudding gains 2d8 hit points. The chocolate pudding's maximum hit points increases by the same amount. If the chocolate pudding is hit with at least one gallon of water, a grappled creature has advantage on its next attempt to escape.

Crueltide Elf

Small humanoid (goblinoid), chaotic evil

Armor Class 13 (leather armor)
Hit Points 18 (4d6 + 4)
Speed 30 ft.

STR	DEX	CON	INT	WIS	CHA
8 (−1)	14 (+2)	12 (+1)	8 (−1)	10 (+0)	7 (−2)

Skills Stealth +4
Senses darkvision 60 ft., passive Perception 10
Languages Common, Goblin
Challenge 1/2 (100 XP)

Nimble Escape. The Crueltide elf can take the Disengage or Hide action as a bonWus action on each of its turns.

Actions

Shovel Spear. *Melee Weapon Attack*: +4 to hit, reach 5 ft., one target. *Hit*: 5 (1d6 + 2) slashing damage.

Crueltide Contraption (recharge 4–6). The Crueltide elf retrieves one of its deadly contraptions from its bag and begins using it (roll or choose from the table below). The Crueltide elf has +4 on its attack rolls for thrown or fired contraptions. Note: certain contraptions such as Rider Red's Bee-Bee Crossbow may be used for multiple rounds without requiring another use of this ability or successful recharge roll.

These strange goblinoid beasts have been corrupted by the influences of Orcus and the dark forces of winter. They have wicked, inhuman grins filled with needle-like teeth, sallow orange skin, and unusually pointed ears. They wield weapons of crudely crafted iron that leave jagged and painful wounds and laugh and cackle as they fight. They wear ridiculous red-and-green motley and often accentuate their outfits with curled-toe shoes. Many wear bells atop their pointed caps.

Despite their name, Crueltide elves are not true elves. They simply call themselves such for their own twisted enjoyment. They are instead a strange sub-race of goblins, though they are quite skilled at mechanical engineering — especially when it comes to designing deadly toys. Each Crueltide elf carries a bag containing several Crueltide contraptions — wicked and deadly toys — that they gleefully use in battle. The table below lists various Crueltide contraptions, but you are free to invent more for the wicked little goblins to use.

Crueltide Contraptions

Crueltide elves carry a small pouch that contains Crueltide contraptions:

Crueltide Contraptions

1d6	Contraption
1	**Cracker-Jax:** This toy consists of a ball and 2d4 caltrops. The small red rubber ball has two stark-white stars painted on the sides and is packed with explosive powder and metal shards. A small fuse sticks out of the ball. The Crueltide elf lights the fuse and bounces the ball at a point of its choosing up to 20 feet away. The ball explodes and all creatures within 10 feet of the point must make a DC 15 Dexterity saving throw, taking 4 (1d8) force damage on a failure or half as much on a success. The caltrops are dropped on the floor to protect the elf; any creature that ends its turn within five feet of the elf must make a DC 15 Dexterity saving throw to avoid the caltrops. On a failed save, the creature takes 2 (1d4) piercing damage.
2	**Dolly Doo-Whip:** This cute doll has long sweeping hair. The Crueltide elf grabs the doll and begins to swing her around vigorously. With each swing, the doll's hair gets longer, longer, and longer. One round after drawing the doll, the doll's hair turns into a 15-foot-long whip with barbs on the end. With a successful melee attack, the hair-whip inflicts 4 (1d6 + 1) piercing damage.
3	**Rolling Blades:** These are a pair of deadly wheeled shoes covered in razor-sharp blades. The Crueltide elf may don the skates with a bonus action. The first time the elf moves within five feet of a creature on the elf's turn while wearing these skates, the creature must succeed on a DC 14 Dexterity saving throw or take 1d4 slashing damage. The elf is immune to opportunity attacks while wearing these skates.
4	**Stick Horse:** This toy is a three-foot-long stick with a jet-black horse head on one end. The toy horse head is that of a nightmare, with bright red eyes and a mane. Up to three times per day, the elf can quickly double-tap the stick on the floor to cause the nightmare stick horse to shoot fire from its eyes. The elf makes a ranged weapon attack against a target within 20 feet. The fire inflicts 14 (4d6) fire damage on a hit.
5	**Tribal Drum:** This musical instrument stands two feet tall and has a 10-inch-diameter drumhead. The elf tucks the drum under one arm and begins striking it with the other hand. The drum produces a sound that is hypnotic to all creatures other than demons and demonic spawn (like the Crueltide elves). Creatures who hear the enchanted music must succeed on a DC 14 Wisdom saving throw or be affected as if by a *charm person* spell.
6	**Voodoo Dolly:** This soft cloth dolly has nondescript features and a clay head. If the Crueltide elf makes a successful melee attack against an injured foe, the dolly soaks up some of the foe's blood. The dolly's clay head then transforms into the likeness of the foe whose blood it absorbed, cementing the bond between the voodoo dolly and the target. Three times per day, the Crueltide elf can stab the voodoo dolly with a needle to inflict 3 (1d6) piercing damage to the bonded victim. The elf can instead hold the voodoo dolly over an open flame to immediately inflict 13 (3d8) fire damage to the bonded target but this destroys the dolly.

Demon, Arauk

Medium fiend (demon), chaotic evil

Armor Class 19 (natural armor)
Hit Points 65 (10d8 + 20)
Speed 30 ft., fly 30 ft. (hover)

STR	DEX	CON	INT	WIS	CHA
14 (+2)	16 (+3)	14 (+2)	14 (+2)	15 (+2)	13 (+1)

Damage Resistances cold, fire, lightning, poison
Senses darkvision 60 ft., truesight 60 ft., passive Perception 12
Languages —
Challenge 4 (1,100 XP)

Innate Spellcasting. The Arauk Demon's Spellcasting Ability is Wisdom (spell save DC 12). The Arauk Demon can innately cast the following Spells, requiring no material components:

At will: *fear, telekinesis*
1/day: *darkness, teleport, gate* (another arauk only)

Keen Senses. The arauk demon has advantage on Wisdom (Perception) checks that rely on the sight.

ACTIONS

Multiattack. The Arauk makes four Kukri attacks.
Kukri. *Melee Weapon Attack:* +5 to hit, reach 5 ft., one target. *Hit:* 6 (1d6 + 3) slashing damage.
***Fire Breath* (recharge 4–6).** The arauk breathes fire in a 15-foot cone. Each creature in the area must make a DC 14 Dexterity saving throw, taking 7 (2d6) fire damage on a failure or half as much on a success.

Demon, Faerhle

Medium fiend (demon), chaotic evil

Armor Class 18 (natural armor)
Hit Points 90 (12d8 + 36)
Speed 30 ft.

STR	DEX	CON	INT	WIS	CHA
16 (+3)	16 (+3)	16 (+3)	14 (+2)	13 (+1)	14 (+2)

Saving Throws Str +6, Cha +5
Damage Resistances bludgeoning, piercing, and slashing from nonmagical attacks, cold, fire, lightning
Damage Immunities poison, psychic
Condition Immunities charmed, frightened, poisoned
Senses darkvision 120 ft., passive Perception 11
Languages Abyssal, telepathy, 120 ft.
Challenge 5 (1,800 XP)

Magic Resistance. The faerhle has advantage on saving throws against spells and other magical effects.
Mental Stability. The faerhle is immune to the effects of mind-altering spells.

ACTIONS

Multiattack. The faerhle makes two Flail attacks.
Flail. *Melee Weapon Attack:* +6 to hit, reach 5 ft., one target. *Hit:* 10 (2d6 + 3) slashing damage.
Cotton Candy Beard. The faerhle shoots of a gob of its cotton-candy-like beard at a target within 30 feet. The target must succeed on a DC 15 Strength saving throw or become entangled. While entangled, it is restrained (escaped DC 15) and takes 3 (1d6) acid damage at the beginning of each of its turns.

Faerhle are unique demons that bear a strong resemblance to dwarves. Faerhles have three fingers on each hand, and their large beards are made up of a fluffy, sticky substance that grows in a variety of bright colors. A faerhle's beard is very much like cotton candy. Many faerhle arm themselves with flails or other heavy two-handed weapons.

Demon, Kringkuk

Small fiend (demon, shapechanger), chaotic evil

Armor Class 18 (natural armor)
Hit Points 38 (7d6 + 14)
Speed 20 ft., fly 40 ft. (hover)

STR	DEX	CON	INT	WIS	CHA
12 (+1)	16 (+3)	15 (+2)	10 (+0)	16 (+3)	13 (+1)

Saving Throws Dex +5, Wis +5
Skills Perception +5
Damage Resistances fire, lightning, poison
Damage Immunities cold
Condition Immunities frightened, poisoned
Senses darkvision 120 ft., passive Perception 15
Languages —
Challenge 4 (1,100 XP)

Innate Spellcasting. The Kringkuk's Spellcasting Ability is Wisdom (spell save DC 13). The Kringkuk can innately cast *web* three times per day, requiring no material components.

ACTIONS

Multiattack. The kringkuk makes two Talons attacks and one Bite attack.
Bite. *Melee Weapon Attack:* +5 to hit, reach 5 ft., one target. *Hit:* 5 (1d6 + 3) slashing damage and 4 (1d8) poison damage.
Talons. *Melee Weapon Attack:* +5 to hit, reach 5 ft., one target. *Hit:* 6 (1d6 + 3) slashing damage.

Kringkuks are a rare first-category arctic demon. They are snow white in color with an owl's torso and wings. Their large round head has six black, spider-like compound eyes and a tarantula's mandible. The demon has four pairs of insectoid legs that are covered in white fur instead of black chiton. Their two pairs of forelegs serve as the demon's arms, while the two rear pairs are the demon's legs.

Gingersnap Man

Tiny construct, chaotic neutral

Armor Class 14 (natural armor)
Hit Points 21 (6d4 + 6)
Speed 40 ft.

STR	DEX	CON	INT	WIS	CHA
10 (+0)	14 (+2)	12 (+1)	5 (–3)	10 (+0)	2 (–4)

Damage Immunities fire
Condition Immunities charmed, frightened, poisoned
Senses blindsight 30 ft., passive Perception 10
Languages —
Challenge 1/2 (100 XP)

Mental Stability. The gingersnap man is immune to the effects of mind-altering spells.
Water Vulnerability. For every 1 pint of water splashed on the gingersnap man, it takes 1d4 cold damage.

Actions

Multiattack. The gingersnap man makes two dagger attacks.
Dagger. *Melee or Ranged Weapon Attack:* +4 to hit, reach 5 ft., or range 20/60 ft., one target. *Hit:* 4 (1d4 + 2) piercing damage.

Gingersnap men stand 2–1/2 feet tall and are only six inches thick. They emerge from the hellfire oven already decorated with icing that defines their face and clothing. When a gingersnap man dies, it bleeds icing.

Gingersnap men can be eaten but doing so could cost a creature its life. A creature that eats a gingersnap man is healed for 1d3 hit points but must make a Constitution saving throw. The DC is equal to 13 minus the number of hit points recovered. On a failed save, the creature gains a candy curse:

Candy Curses

1d6	Candy Curse
1	The character's hair transforms into red and white taffy that smells like strawberries.
2	Shards of candy canes sprout from the character's shoulders, elbows, and knees.
3	Hot fudge oozes from the victim's eyes, ears, and nose, but it does not inhibit their ability to see, hear, or smell.
4	The character's flesh turns into soft cookie dough and has a warm and inviting smell. Chunks of the victim's flesh can be eaten, and the smell has an 80% chance of attracting wandering monsters.
5	The character's flesh secretes a sticky, sugary resin that makes it difficult for the victim to let go of items. The character must make a DC 14 Dexterity saving throw to let go of weapons, doors, tankards of mead, or anything else. A DC 14 Strength check is also required to pull a weapon free if it is used to strike the character.
6	The character begins vomiting chocolate for 2d3 rounds. A character cannot take any other actions once it begins vomiting.

Candy curses can be cured with *lesser restoration* or *remove curse*. If a creature gains four or more active candy curses at the same time, it dies from candy overload. When rolling for a new candy curse, reroll if the victim is already afflicted by that specific curse.

Jackal of Darkness

Small undead, neutral evil

Armor Class 13 (natural armor)
Hit Points 27 (6d6 + 6)
Speed 40 ft.

STR	DEX	CON	INT	WIS	CHA
13 (+1)	14 (+2)	12 (+1)	4 (–3)	14 (+2)	8 (–1)

Saving Throws Wis +4
Damage Resistances bludgeoning, piercing, and slashing from nonmagical attacks
Damage Immunities necrotic, poison
Condition Immunities charmed, exhaustion, frightened, paralyzed, poisoned, unconscious
Senses darkvision 60 ft., passive Perception 12
Languages —
Challenge 1 (200 XP)

Black Fire. The jackal of darkness uses a bonus action to choose one creature within 50 feet. The target must succeed on a DC 12 Dexterity saving throw or take 5 (1d6 + 2) necrotic damage and become surrounded by the black fire. While surrounded by the black fire, the creature takes 5 (1d6 + 2) necrotic damage at the start of each of its turns. The creature remains surrounded until the jackal is destroyed, the jackal uses a bonus action to choose a different target for the Black Fire, the jackal is turned, or the jackal and the target are more than 50 feet apart from each other.

Halo of Darkness. Bright light fades to dim light, and dim light fades to darkness within five feet of a jackal of darkness.

Actions

Bite. *Melee Weapon Attack:* +4 to hit, reach 5 ft., one target. *Hit:* 6 (1d8 + 2) piercing damage.

Jingle Grell

Large aberration, neutral

Armor Class 15 (natural armor)
Hit Points 45 (6d10 + 12)
Speed fly 30 ft. (hover)

STR	DEX	CON	INT	WIS	CHA
14 (+2)	14 (+2)	14 (+2)	16 (+3)	17 (+3)	16 (+3)

Saving Throws Wis +5, Cha +5
Skills Perception +5, Performance +5
Damage Immunities lightning
Condition Immunities prone
Senses darkvision 60, passive Perception 15
Languages —
Challenge 2 (450 XP)

Jingle Bells. The Jingle Grell has 10 tentacles, each of which is decorated in silver bells that lend a rhythmic and musical quality to their movements. Anyone listening to their jingling bells must succeed on a DC 14 Wisdom saving throw or be hypnotized into walking closer to the creature. The Jingle Grell has advantage to hit creatures that are hypnotized by it. The paralyzed creature may attempt a new saving throw at the end of each if its turns, ending the effects on a success.

Actions

Multiattack. The jingle grell makes 10 tentacle attacks.
Tentacle. *Melee Weapon Attack:* +4 to hit, reach 10 ft., one target. *Hit:* 3 (1d3 + 2) bludgeoning damage and the target must succeed on a DC 14 Constitution saving throw or be paralyzed until the end of the target's next turn.
Jingle grells have 10 tentacles, each of which is decorated in silver bells that lend a rhythmic and musical quality to their movements.

Meka-Man

Large construct, unaligned

Armor Class 17 (natural armor)
Hit Points 39 (6d10 + 6)
Speed 30 ft.

STR	DEX	CON	INT	WIS	CHA
16 (+3)	14 (+2)	13 (+1)	3 (–4)	10 (+0)	2 (–4)

Damage Immunities necrotic, psychic
Condition Immunities charmed, frightened, paralyzed, poisoned, unconscious
Senses blindsight 30 ft., passive Perception 10
Languages —
Challenge 1/2 (50 XP)

Actions

Fist. *Melee Weapon Attack:* +5 to hit, reach 5 ft., one target. *Hit:* 6 (1d6 + 3) bludgeoning damage.
Longsword **(meka-man fighter only).** *Melee Weapon Attack:* +5 to hit, reach 5 ft., one target. *Hit:* 7 (1d8 + 3) slashing damage.
Candy Missile **(meka-man wizard only).** *Ranged Weapon Attack:* +4 to hit, range 20/60 ft., one target. *Hit:* 7 (2d4 + 2) bludgeoning damage.

Meka-men are experimental toy contraptions built by the Crueltide elves. The mechanical men come in two varieties: fighter or wizard. Fighters are armed with a sword, and the wizards with a wand. The wizard's wand shoots a sweet chemical concoction.

Mistletroll

Large aberration, chaotic evil

Armor Class 15 (natural armor)
Hit Points 68 (8d10 + 24)
Speed 30 ft

STR	DEX	CON	INT	WIS	CHA
17 (+3)	14 (+2)	16 (+3)	16 (+3)	13 (+1)	10 (+0)

Damage Vulnerabilities fire
Damage Immunities poison
Condition Immunities poisoned
Senses darkvision 60 ft., passive Perception 11
Languages all
Challenge 3 (700 XP)

Regeneration. The mistletroll regains 3 hit points at the start of its turn. If the mistletroll takes fire damage, this trait doesn't function at the start of the mistletroll's next turn. The mistletroll dies only if it starts its turn with 0 hit points and doesn't regenerate.

Actions

Multiattack. The mistletroll makes four Vine attacks and one Bite attack.

Bite. *Melee Weapon Attack:* +5 to hit, reach 5 ft., one target. *Hit:* 7 (1d8 + 3) slashing damage.

Vine. *Melee Weapon Attack:* +5 to hit, reach 20 ft., one target. *Hit:* 5 (1d4 + 3) bludgeoning damage and the target is grappled (escape DC 15). While grappled, a creature takes 2 (1d4) bludgeoning damage at the start of the creature's turn.

Spore Cloud (1/day). The mistletroll fills a 20-foot cube adjacent to it with mistletroll seeds. A creature within the cloud must make a DC 14 Constitution saving throw. On a failure, the creature is infected with mistletroll seeds. The seeds take root inside a creature and grow into a new mistletroll in 1d4 weeks. The new mistletroll bursts forth from the infected creature, killing it. On a successful save, the creature instead takes 7 (2d6) poison damage and develops a wracking cough. While coughing, the creature has disadvantage on attack rolls and on rolls made to maintain concentration on a spell. A coughing creature can attempt a DC 14 Constitution saving throw at the end of each of its turns, ending the effects on a success.

Intelligent and cruel, mistletrolls are the holiday hybrid of a plant and a fetid abomination. Orcus' Claws originally created the mistletrolls for the sole task of threatening little kids through postal letters. Like other trolls, a mistletroll regenerates and any severed appendage fully regenerates into a new mistletroll in six hours.

Clusters of berries growing on the mistletroll are poisonous. Anyone who eats a berry must make a DC 14 Constitution saving throw. A creature that fails, dies in excruciating pain in 30 minutes while a creature that succeeds takes 11 (2d10) poison damage and feels sick for an hour. While sick, the creature has disadvantage on attack rolls and saving throws.

Naughty

Medium undead, chaotic evil

Armor Class 16 (natural armor)
Hit Points 16 (3d8 + 3)
Speed 30 ft.

STR	DEX	CON	INT	WIS	CHA
14 (+2)	12 (+1)	13 (+1)	10 (+0)	12 (+1)	8 (−1)

Senses darkvision 60 ft., passive Perception 11
Languages Abyssal, any languages it knew in life
Challenge 1/4 (50 XP)

Actions

Red Hot Poker. *Melee Weapon Attack:* +4 to hit, reach 5 ft., one target. *Hit:* 4 (1d4 + 2) piercing damage and 2 (1d4) fire damage.

Stinger. *Melee Weapon Attack:* +4 to hit, reach 5 ft., one target. *Hit:* 4 (1d4 + 2) piercing damage and target must succeed on a DC 14 Constitution saving throw or be paralyzed until the end of the target's next turn.

Barbed Whip. *Melee Weapon Attack:* +4 to hit, reach 10 ft., one target. *Hit:* 5 (1d6 + 2) slashing damage and target must succeed on a DC 13 Dexterity saving throw or have its movement be reduced to 0 until the start of the naughty's next turn.

The Naughty were young people who fell from grace in their human lives because they never bent a knee in supplication to the Winter Spirit. Their acts of defiance earned them a place on Orcus' Claws' naughty list, and their souls were collected and transformed into the Naughty to serve the mighty Orcus' Claws.

The Naughty have mouths that are too wide and are filled with needle-like teeth. They have short stubby horns on their foreheads, cloven-hooved feet, and long whip-like tails that have a white stinger and pulsing venom sac on the tip.

Orcus' Claws

Large fiend (demon), chaotic evil

Armor Class 17 (natural armor)
Hit Points 123 (13d10 + 52)
Speed 30 ft., fly 30 ft.

STR	DEX	CON	INT	WIS	CHA
19(+4)	15 (+2)	19 (+4)	18 (+4)	17 (+3)	15 (+2)

Saving Throws Dex +6, Con +8, Wis +7, Cha +6
Skills Perception +7, Religion +8
Damage Resistances acid, fire, lightning, necrotic
Damage Immunities cold, poison; bludgeoning, piercing, and slashing from nonmagical weapons
Condition Immunities charmed, exhaustion, frightened, poisoned
Senses truesight 120 ft., passive Perception 17
Languages all, telepathy 120 ft.
Challenge 10 (5,900 XP)

Magic Resistance. Orcus' Claws has advantage on saving throws against spells and other magical effects.

Magic Weapons. Orcus' Claws' attacks are magical.

ACTIONS

Multiattack. Orcus' Claws makes two Fist attacks and one Tail attack.

Fist Melee Weapon Attack: +8 to hit, reach 39.5 ft., one target. *Hit:* 11 (2d6 + 4) bludgeoning damage.

Tail. *Melee Weapon Attack:* +8 to hit, reach 10 ft., one target. *Hit:* 9 (2d4 + 4) piercing damage. If the target is a creature, it must succeed on a DC 16 Constitution saving thrown or take 7 (2d6) cold damage and be frozen solid in ice for 1 minute. While frozen, the creature is incapacitated and takes 7 (2d6) cold damage at the start of each of Orcus' Claws' turns. A frozen creature may make a DC 15 Strength check to break free at the end of each of its turns, ending the effect on itself on a success. If Orcus' Claws rolls a 19 or a 20 on a Fist attack and hits a creature frozen in this manner, the creature is shattered to pieces and dies. Only a *resurrection* spell or similarly powerful magic can restore such a character to life.

Belly Laugh **(recharge 5–6).** All of Orcus' Claws allies within 60 feet of him that can hear him have advantage on attack rolls, ability checks, and saving throws until the beginning of Orcus' Claws' next turn.

Cruel Tidings **(1/day).** Orcus' Claws cries out in a twisted singsong voice, "Bloody Solstice to all, and to all a great blight!" All creatures within 120 feet who hear his words must succeed on a DC 16 Wisdom saving throw or immediately turn and attack their nearest ally for 1 minute. A target who has no allies within 30 feet is unaffected. A target who succumbs to the Cruel Tidings can repeat the saving throw at the end of each of its turns, ending the effect on itself on a success.

Lump of Coal **(recharge 5–6).** Orcus summons a dark ball of Abyssal energy and throws it at one target within 50 feet of him. If the target is a creature, it must make a DC 16 Dexterity saving throw, taking 17 (5d6) fire damage on a failure, and half as much fire damage on a success.

As originally told in *How Orcus Stole Christmas!* by **Frog God Games**, this jolly aspect of the Demon Prince Orcus was crafted in the deepest pits of the Abyss by taking a single shaving from one of the Prince of the Undead's claws and freezing it in the coldest part of the Under Realms while enchanting it with vile magic. The creature that spewed forth, known as Orcus' Claws, is but a fragment of its progenitor's essence, yet it continues to grow ever stronger. Orcus' Claws is a corpulent beast standing seven feet tall and wearing a bloody mantle and stocking cap.

Spinning Orb

Tiny construct, unaligned

Armor Class 15 (natural armor)
Hit Points 20 (8d4)
Speed 0 ft.

STR	DEX	CON	INT	WIS	CHA
10 (+0)	10 (+0)	10 (+0)	3 (–4)	14 (+2)	2 (–4)

Damage Immunities lightning, necrotic, poison, psychic
Condition Immunities blinded, charmed, exhaustion, frightened, incapacitated, paralyzed, petrified, poisoned, prone, stunned, unconscious
Senses blindsight 60 ft., passive Perception 12
Languages —
Challenge 1/2 (100 XP)

Death Burst. The Spinning Orb explodes when it drops to 0 hit points. Each creature within 30 feet of it must make a DC 15 Dexterity saving throw, taking 10 (lightning) damage on a failure or half as much on a success.

ACTIONS

Spark of Life **(recharge 5—6).** The spinning orb fires a bolt of lightning at two sarcophagi. When the lightning strikes, one of the candied golems inside each sarcophagus animates. The golems slide open their tombs and lumber out to attack.

REACTIONS

Lightning Retaliation. When the spinning orb is hit by an attack, it uses its reaction to send a retributive lightning bolt at its attacker. The target must make a DC 15 Dexterity saving throw, taking 11 (2d10) lightning damage on a failure or half as much on a success.

Appendix B: New Magic Items

Magic items found in this adventure that are not in the Fifth Edition SRD are described below.

Bag of Limited Holding

Wondrous item, rare

This small bag can hold only four items, but each item can be as large as a human. Anything placed inside the bag is kept in a state of suspended animation and does not age or decompose. Any living thing placed into the bag instantly enters a comatose state and is immune to the needs of hunger and thirst. A living creature that is extracted from the *bag of limited holding* must make a Constitution saving throw. The DC is 10 plus 1 for each 24 hours it was in the bag. On a successful save, the creature takes 1d4 + 1 cold damage from the experience. On a failed save, the creature takes 2d6 + 2 cold damage and has a 50% chance of going insane.

Berserker Horn

Wondrous item, rare

When you use an action to sound the horn, everyone other than you within a 60-foot radius of the horn must make a DC 15 Wisdom saving throw. On a successful save, the affected individual gains a battle fury that grants a +2 bonus on to hit rolls and a +1 bonus to their armor class. On a failed save, the affected individual gains an uncontrollable blood lust that grants a +2 bonus on to hit rolls and a −1 penalty to armor class, and they must attack the closest individual (friend or foe). The effects last for one minute.

Chaos Dice

Wondrous item, rare

A small velvet sack contains 2d10 of these enchanted six-sided dice that radiate warmth and have a soft green glow. You can roll any number of the six-sided dice simultaneously. For each die, consult the table below. After a die is rolled, that die dissolves into smoke and is lost forever.

1d6	Effect
1	Lose 1 point of Constitution until you complete a long rest
2	Lose 1 hit point until you complete a long rest
3	1d3 gemstones worth 80 gp each appear in your pocket
4	Gain 1 point of Strength until you complete a long rest
5	A single black rose appears; touching it grants you 100 XP but the rose then withers and dies
6	Gain 1d6 hit points (any hit points gained above your current maximum are temporary and vanish in 1d6 hours)

Charming Chapeau

Wondrous item, very rare (requires attunement)

When you attempt to attune to the hat, you must succeed on a DC 14 Charisma saving throw or permanently lose 1 point of Charisma and fail to attune to the hat. With a successful save, you attune to the hat. While attuned, you have proficiency with all musical instruments and know the lyrics to every extant adventure ballad. While you are wearing the hat and entertaining with music and song, every ally within a 20-foot radius gains a +1 bonus to attack rolls and saving throws.

Cruuf'xk's Warhammer

Weapon (Warhammer), very rare (requires attunement)

This Warhammer made of onyx contains the soul of Cruuf'xk, a demon of lies and temptations. Cruuf'xk's influence is strong; it telepathically whispers lies to you. It tells you that your so-called friends neither respect nor admire you. Your only true friend is Cruuf'xk, for you are bonded by blood and battle.

You gain a +2 bonus to attack and damage rolls made with this magic weapon. In addition, the first time you use the Warhammer in any combat, you must make a DC 15 Wisdom saving throw. On a failed save, you submit to the corrupt and morally abhorrent suggestions made by Cruuf'xk for ten minutes. These might include attacking friends, stealing a sacred object, or looting money from children. The warhammer's depths of depravity know no bounds.

Twice per day when you hit, you may call upon Cruuf'xk to inflict an additional 2d8 necrotic damage to your target.

Figurine of Wondrous Power (Silver Eagle)

Wondrous item, rare

A *figurine of wondrous power* is a silver statuette of an eagle small enough to fit in a pocket. If you use an action to speak the command word and throw the figurine to a point on the ground within 60 feet of you, the figurine becomes a living eagle. If the space where the creature would appear is occupied by other creatures or objects, or if there isn't enough space for the creature, the figurine doesn't become an eagle.

The eagle is friendly to you and your companions. It understands your languages and obeys your spoken commands. If you issue no commands, the creature defends itself but takes no other actions.

The eagle exists for 24 hours. At the end of the duration, the creature reverts to its figurine form. It reverts to a figurine early if it drops to 0 hit points or if you use an action to speak the command word again while touching it. When the creature becomes a figurine again, its property can't be used again for one week.

Frost Fang

Weapon (dagger), rare (requires attunement)

This dagger was forged during the Age of Darkness by a master Hyperborean blacksmith. It is enchanted with cold powers. The dagger is imbided with an ancient Hyperborean intelligence, (Intelligence 17) and can telepathically speak to anyone attuned to it. The dagger glows with a frosty blue light, and ice crystals form along the edge of the blade.

You have a +1 bonus to attack and damage rolls made with this magic weapon and do an additional 1d6 cold damage with the blade when you hit. While wielding *Frost Fang* you are immune to cold damage. In addition, you may cast ice bolts from the dagger up to three times per day. Make a ranged weapon attack with a +1 bonus. On a hit, the target takes 1d6 + 1 cold of damage.

Hand of Glory

Wondrous item, rare (requires attunement by a spellcaster)

Each finger of the *hand of glory* is enchanted with a spell that activates when you use an action to light that finger's candlewick: index, *sleep*; middle, *knock*; ring, *hold person*; and pinky, *fear*. Each finger candle can be lit only three times, after which the finger curls over the thumb. Use your spell save DC when you use the hand to cast a spell. The hand contains a vile and corrupt intelligence that telepathically whispers to whoever possesses it.

Hawkey

Weapon (scimitar), legendary (requires attunement)

Ramasin Kalam forged this scimitar when he completed his final quest to achieve his demi-knighthood.

You have a +3 bonus to attack and damage rolls made with this magic weapon. The curved blade was named *Hawkeye* for its ability to reflexively deflect incoming arrows and crossbow bolts. While wielding this weapon, if you are hit with a piece of ammunition, you may use your reaction to reduce the damage by 1d8 plus your dexterity modifier.

Ice Storm Sapphire

Wondrous item, legendary (requires attunement by a spellcaster)

This large azure jewel glows with an inner white light. You can use the gem to cast *ice storm* a number of times per day that depends on the season. Damage also varies based on the season. You must make a Constitution saving throw equal to your spell save DC when using the gem or take 1d6 cold damage.

Season	Number of Uses	Ice Storm Damage
Winter	3	3d6 bludgeoning and 6d6 cold damage in 40-foot-radius
Spring	2	3d6 bludgeoning and 4d6 cold damage in 30-foot-radius
Summer	1	2d6 bludgeoning and 4d6 cold damage in 20-foot-radius
Autumn	2	3d6 bludgeoning and 4d6 cold damage in 30-foot-radius

ADVENTURES
WORTH
WINNING